Alvin Krinst

The

Yalta

Stunts

Edited and with an Introduction by

Emily MacGregor

© 1989, 1993 by The Institute of Krinst Studies
© 2016 by Sagging Meniscus Press

All Rights Reserved.

Printed in the United States of America.

ISBN: 978-0-9861445-2-3 (paperback)
Library of Congress Control Number: 2016934033

Sagging Meniscus Press
web: http://www.saggingmeniscus.com/
email: info@saggingmeniscus.com

The Yalta Stunts

Introduction

When Stalin, Churchill, and Roosevelt set the date for their historic conference at Yalta in late 1944, it seemed natural to include in their plans a series of elaborate stunts that would refresh their minds and keep their bodies active during the long hours of thoughtful scrutiny and political bargaining. Diversions such as charades and musical chairs had become immensely popular among the Allied High Command as early as 1942, and by the time of the Soviet capture of Lutsk in February 1943, more complicated amusements had become *de rigeur* for all major conferences. At the Quadrant Conference of August 11-24, 1943, for example, during the discussion of operation OVERLORD the U.S. Chiefs of Staff had managed to construct an immense pyramid of champagne glasses while simultaneously asserting that a vigorous Italian campaign was essential to draw off German strength. Roosevelt himself had balanced a plum on his nose to demonstrate his gratitude when Churchill suggested that a U.S. officer lead the cross-Channel attack. At the Moscow Conference of October 1943, Molotov and Eden had dressed like ministers and shouted rude insults at passers-by, and U.S. Secretary of State Cordell Hull had, on a dare, run naked through Red Square carrying a piglet and singing patriotic songs.

By 1944, however, some of this high-spiritedness had lost its charm, and the three giants decided that a radical change in the quality and character of these "strategy stunts" was needed. Stalin wanted more mentally engaging stunts—mathematical puzzles and logical games—while Churchill thought that the new stunts should involve a lot of squeaky noises and pot-banging. It was Roosevelt, however, who proposed the idea of commissioning a series of stunts from an internationally known artist or philosopher. This person would have to be a genius of rare quality, able to blend poignancy and rigorous intellectual discipline with a sense of silliness equal to the magnitude of the event.

None was more surprised, perhaps, than Krinst himself at the invitation to author these Yalta stunts. He had been aware of the war only insofar as he was frustrated at his inability to get good chocolate, and knew little of contemporary political matters, save that his landlord who professed Nazi sympathies was unable to tie his shoes or wash himself. He recognized only Stalin's name (they had met in the 1920's, possibly at the Kiev international plumber's convention of 1926), and, because he initially thought Roosevelt was an old school chum whose copy of *Tess of the D'Urbervilles* he had never returned, didn't answer the request for some months. Only when attempting to purchase tickets for a spring cruise along the Rhine did everything fall into place. He wrote immediately and shortly thereafter commenced work on what would be one of his mightiest and most enigmatic texts.

The stunts proved to be ample fruits of Krinst's unswerving, unnerving genius, combining political savvy (he brushed up quickly on current events by screening old newsreels and cartoon shorts on a rented projector) with playful aplomb, mixing mystic symbolism and old-fashioned fun in their often confounding demands. The unique presentation of the stunts was similarly novel; the directions for each activity were accompanied—on the facing page—by a puzzling imperative and an illustration, both of which seemed to hold a curiously anagogic relationship with the stunt itself. Above all, the stunts provided an atmosphere that enabled the three mighty lions to divide the world fairly among themselves—a context of the solvable for the often most rubbery of problems, suggesting merely that all that was needed to solve the most intricate political conundrums was a bit of dexterity, some imagination, and a few household items. All three leaders later declared that without Krinst's stunts they would have been reduced to mean-spirited petty bickering and small-minded power struggles without care or concern for the millions of human lives they were controlling.

The actual text of *The Yalta Stunts* was not made public until 1958, as was Krinst's name; in keeping with the ultra-secret nature of the conference, he had been referred to only by the codename "Substitute." Immediate publication was delayed for some years as Krinst, interpreting certain government communications, thought he was being accused of Communist sympathies and went into hiding. After some clarification and a large cash settlement, however, the first edition appeared in 1963.

Due to the often cryptic nature of the texts, early attempts to recreate the stunts can only be described as brave failures. It was not until the second edition appeared in 1967—with detailed descriptions of how the stunts had been interpreted and performed by Stalin, Churchill, and Roosevelt themselves—that the full splendor of this work came to be realized. Without a doubt the combination of global tension and overwhelming significance that surrounded their enactment, together with the regal personalities of those three great men, provided the force and inspiration for what can truly be called a definitive production of the stunts. Indeed, so much have the original interpretations been accepted that they can hardly be separated from Krinst's work at all, and one might say with some conviction that *The Yalta Stunts*, as it stands today, is the work of *four* great minds working in awesome synchrony. Few modern performances have been anything but strictly adhesive to the Yaltic reading, and the virtues of the occasional departure (such as Ernesto Zingarelli's one-man marathon in 1979) are of but occasional insight, and do not approach the sustained profundity of tradition.

The first commentaries, it should be noted, were most faulty. Not only were they rife with rumor and misinformation, but, more gravely, were edited and exaggerated versions, the results of frenzied nationalism. Soviet editions greatly overstated Stalin's physical prowess and included fraudulent anecdotes in which the two Western leaders compared their own achievements with the Soviet's in obsequious terms; "it is a truism," Churchill was claimed to have said, "that Joseph Stalin's exertions are to be called the most triumphant; ours are but lowly hijinks." British versions tended to downplay what is best called Churchill's extremely whimsical nature. The details of his enthusiastic and varied repetitions of Stunt IV were suppressed to the point of exclusion. U.S. editions were no better. They generally marginalized Stalin's contributions, referring to him often by demeaning epithets, characterized Churchill as a well-meaning but uptight booby, and all but stated explicitly that Roosevelt had run the event like some comico-military wizard, a kind of Harpo Eisenhower in an atomic rocket sled.

In preparing the commentary for this edition, then, I have made every effort to provide an accurate description of the Yaltic interpretations. Where little evidence has existed, or reports have varied widely, I have not speculated. In a few cases, I have uncovered new information, or have corrected long unquestioned errors. My approach has otherwise been traditional, to give a short explanation of each stunt, more or less anecdotal as necessary, with an aim at providing a concise, codified version of these excellent stunts. I have allowed myself the occasional judgmental remark.

Finally, I wish to thank Mr. Walter Smart for his assistance in negotiating the loan of certain Soviet documents, without which this edition would be much impoverished.

Emily MacGregor
August 1989

The Stunts

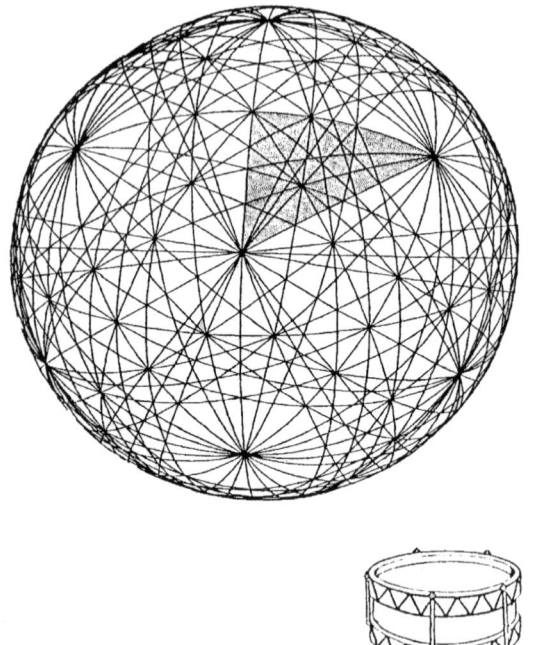

KEEP THE FAITH!

I

Gargle while demonstrating knottings for the necktie.

COMMENTARY

Stalin's performance of this stunt was remarkable; after commencing with a Windsor and a few other basic knots, he managed a double Turkish Twist with one hand.

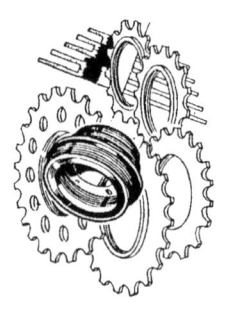

BREATHE EASY!

II

Prepare *Paradise Lost* as a dessert for eating.

COMMENTARY

Stalin used maple syrup, whipped cream, and a cherry; this slightly odd version of a traditionally American preparation has frequently been read as a friendly overture to Roosevelt.

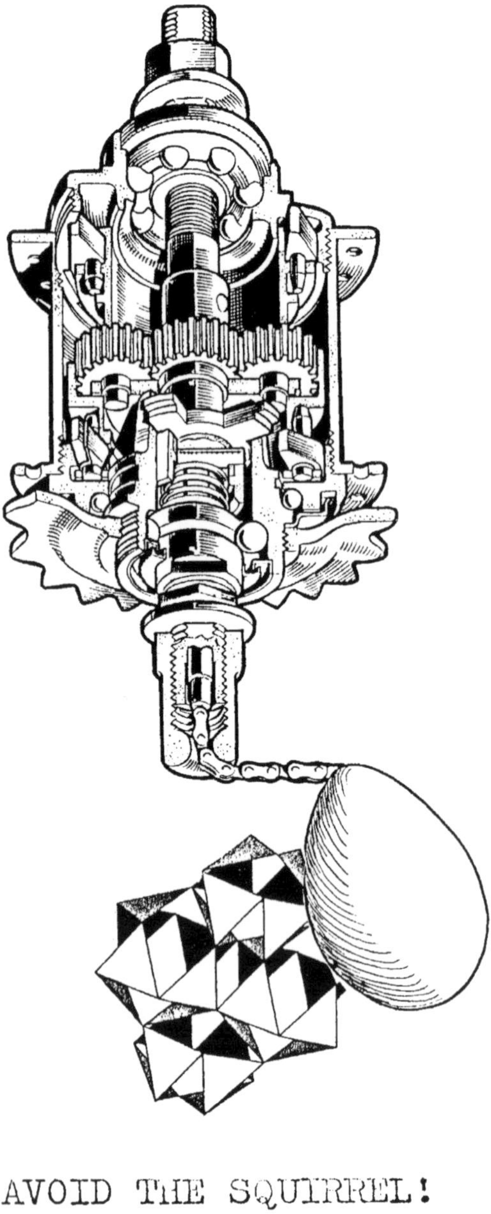

AVOID THE SQUIRREL!

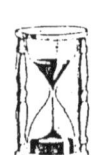

III

Feign amusement at the presentation of a leg.

COMMENTARY

Churchill managed a wan smile and a few convincing chuckles as Stalin rolled up his left pantleg, exposing the limb to the knee.

FLUSH THE INFERIOR

FANCY!

IV

Do the chicken walk.

COMMENTARY

Churchill took to this stunt with characteristic zeal, squatting, flapping his arms, and jerking his head awkwardly. He gave several varied interpretations and would perhaps have gone on for hours had he not strained a muscle while pretending to eat a beetle.

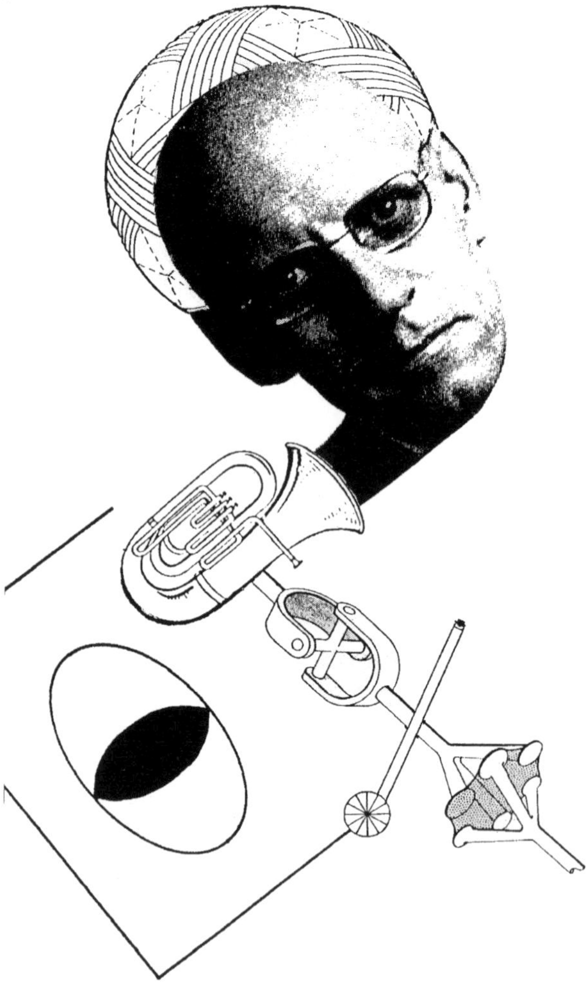

ERECT A MONOLITH OF

MARZIPAN!

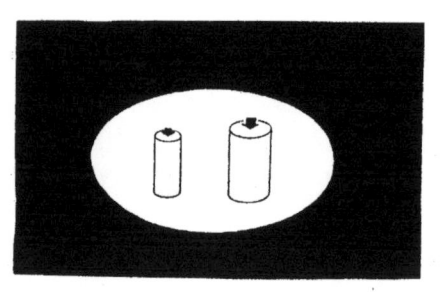

V

Submit a bust of Dante to a religious inquisition.

COMMENTARY

Roosevelt spent some hours berating a small marble likeness of the Florentine poet, demanding that it admit to certain unspeakable heresies, such as attempting to baptise a moose and cheating on catechisms. Toward the end of the performance, he did an excellent impersonation of Mussolini and threatened the bust with torture.

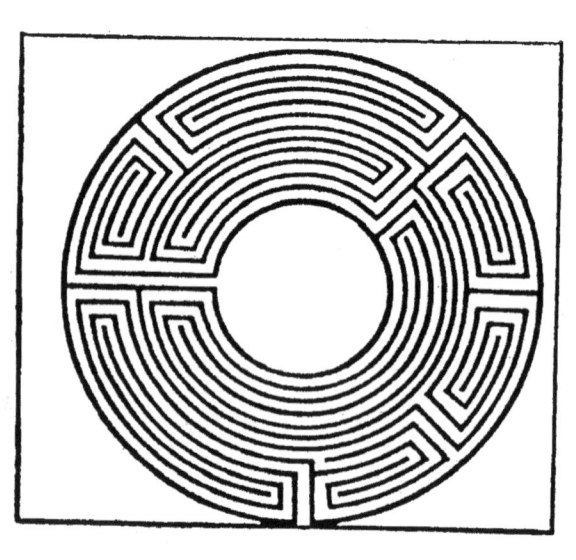

HAVE A HEART ATTACK
THE FRENCH WAY!

VI

Eat x spoonfuls of tapioca at timepoint x where x runs through the series whose first three elements are (1, 2, 3) and whose every subsequent element is the sum of the two preceding.

COMMENTARY

After two minutes had been agreed upon as the length of the time period, Roosevelt commenced this stunt with enthusiasm; he expressed his intention to continue the stunt indefinitely, but sadly died before this was possible.

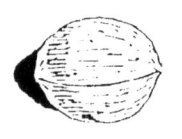

GUESS YOUR WEIGHT!

VII

Run out into the streets to find by buying nuts one who seeks truth.

COMMENTARY

After contemplating for some while, Stalin rushed from the conference rooms and spent the equivalent of thirty-two U.S. dollars on cashews and brazils before overhearing a conversation in which a young woman expressed her desire to know the price of a kilo of figs.

GO TO THE ANT!

வாசித்துவருகையில், ஒவ்வொரு வாக்கியத்தையும் அதற்குரிய படத்தோடு ஒப்பிட்டுப் பார்க்கும் தோறும் அர்த்தமாகிக்கொண்டு வரும். மனப்பாடம் பண்ணிக்கொள்ள வேண்டிய அம்சங்கள் மிகக் குறைவு. ஆகையினால் அர்த்தத்துக்கு இணங்க வாக்கிய அமைப்பின் வேறுபாடுகளோக் கண்டறிந்து கொள்வதற்கு வசதிகள் உண்டு. இம்முறை அஞ்சிரித்து ஆங்கிலம் கற்றுக்கொள்வது கஷ்டமில்லாத ஒருமன் டிவினேயாட்டுச் சம்பந்தப்பட்டது.

VIII

Demolish china; describe it otherwise.

COMMENTARY

Smashing a complete set of fine English tableware with a hammer, Churchill simultaneously delivered a convincing monologue in which he claimed to be preparing *duck à l'orange*, meticulously describing each blow as some step in the culinary process.

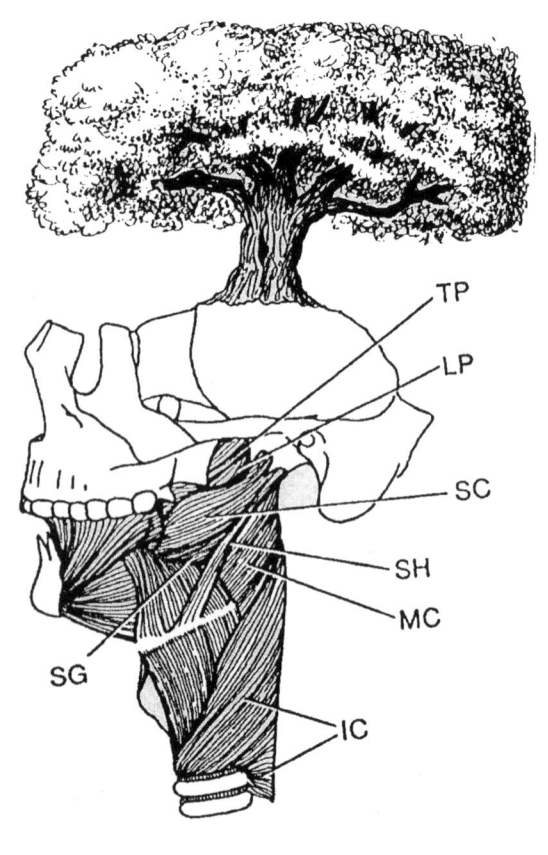

NUDGE A TWEEZER!

เรียนภาษาอังกฤษด้วยภาพ
เมื่อท่านเรียนตามวิธีนี้ไปได้ ๓๐ หน้า ลอง
ทวนความรู้ของท่านดูด้วยการหัดตอบ คำถาม
เป็นภาษาอังกฤษในหน้า ๓๑, ๓๒ และ ๓๓
แล้วพลิกไปตรวจดูคำตอบในหน้า ๓๔ ว่าถูก
ต้องหรือไม่ คำถามและคำตอบมีให้ไว้ต่อๆ
ไปตลอดทั้งเล่ม

IX

Alphabetize sardines.

COMMENTARY

Producing a tin of Norwegian sardines, Stalin opened it and picked out the small fish, giving each one a name as he did so. He then arranged them in the prescribed manner, and ate the one he had dubbed "Gregory."

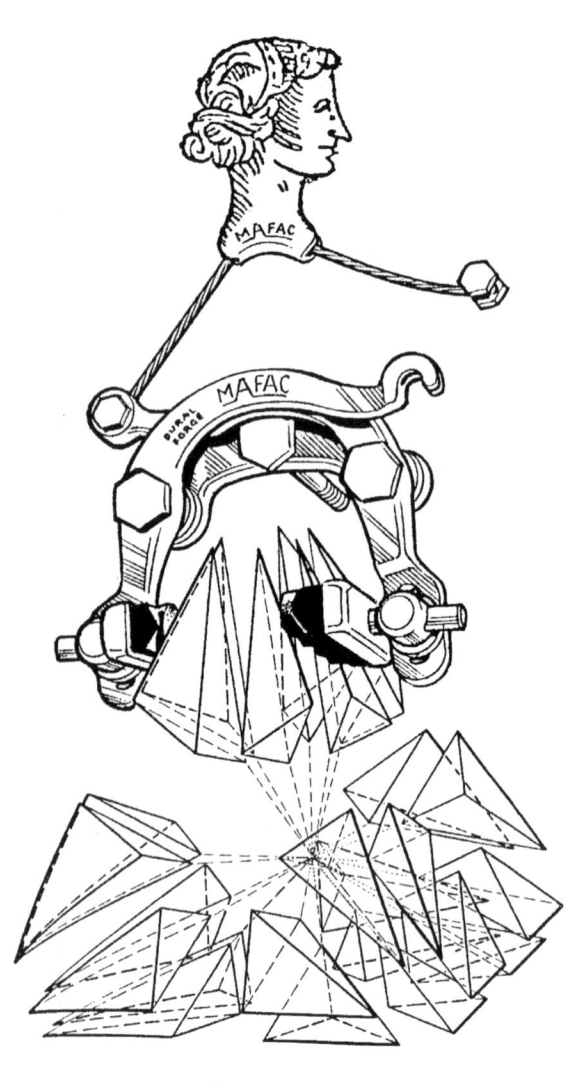

SWEAT MALLETS!

X

Hide but blow a whistle.

COMMENTARY

Some discussion was needed to set out the rules for this stunt before Churchill ran from the room, leaving Roosevelt and Stalin to count to a hundred. Apparently, Churchill was required to blow a small tin whistle once in every ten-minute period he was stationary. If he was moving, this interval was shortened to twenty seconds. Stalin eventually located the Prime Minister in a pantry.

LOSE YOUR MARBLES!

XI

Imitate water in its passage from pond to teacup.

COMMENTARY

Roosevelt took this stunt to entail a kind of mime, and performed expressive motions indicative of bobbing, evaporating, raining, flowing, sitting, flowing, pouring, boiling, steeping, being poured, and, finally (a bonus), being drunk.

ALIENATE CORN!

XII

Box lettuce.

COMMENTARY

Stalin took seriously the opportunity to display his pugilistic skills. Churchill and Roosevelt, however, declared the first round a tie. The robust head of romaine took several uppercuts in the second but held on. Stalin took it in five.

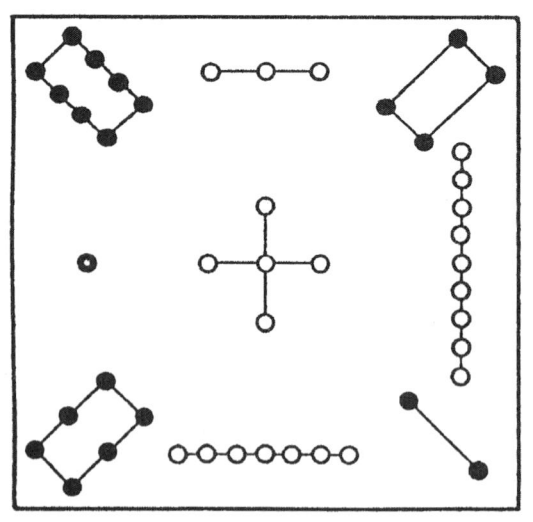

CROWN THE SHADOW!

XIII

List your pains.

COMMENTARY

Taking this stunt literally, Roosevelt proceeded to describe in minute detail the minor aches and irritations of his body. Commentators have frequently glossed this as an admirable admission of fallibility.

CARRY YOUR OWN DOOR!

XIV

While drawing a rabbit, sing "By the Rocks of Loch Lomond."

COMMENTARY

Churchill would not admit that he knew no such song, and improvised several humorous verses to a somewhat wavering tune. He managed a clumsy yet strangely compelling hare.

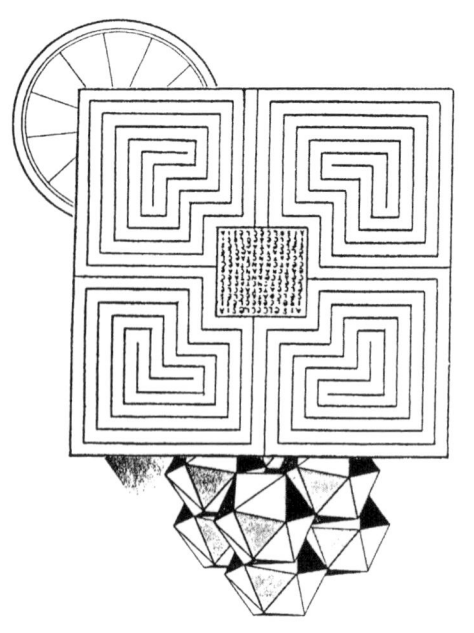

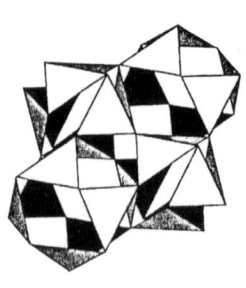

SUCK THAT FAUCET DRY!

XV

Gesticulate while undressing a piano with your eyes.

COMMENTARY

Roosevelt ogled a Steinway furiously and made several odd motions.

എൻജിന്

EXCORIATE AN EDAM!

XVI

Speak a second language to the ceiling.

COMMENTARY

Roosvelt's miserable French accent was the cause of much hilarity as he asked politely for a room with a bath.

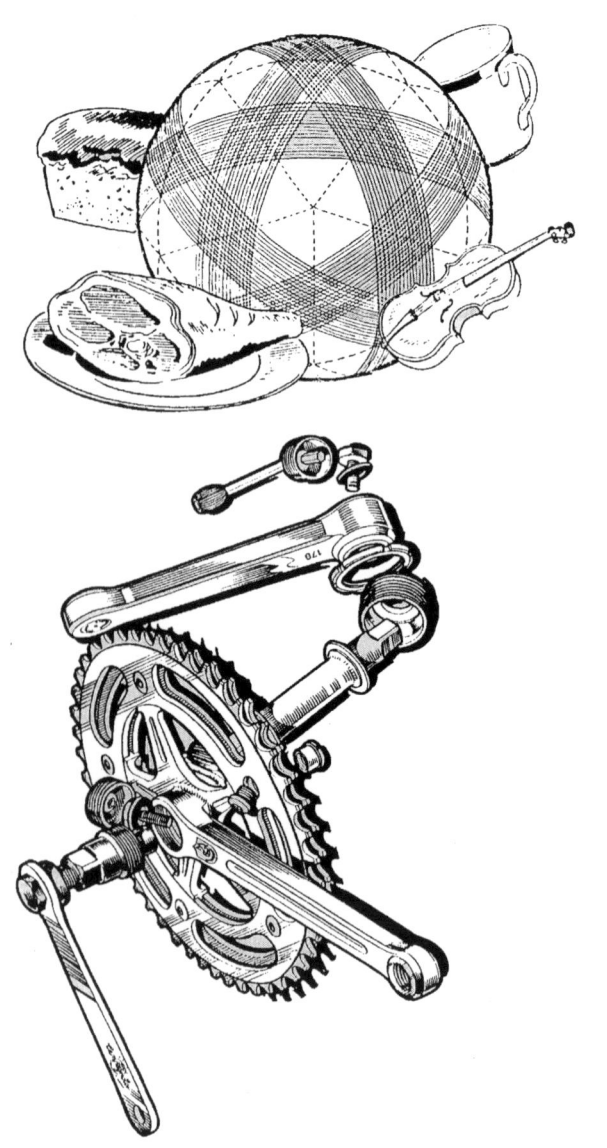

FIND THE WRONG
ONE FOR YOU!

XVII

Repeat Keats while balancing a dictionary on your head.

COMMENTARY

Initially, Stalin thought to impress his co-stunters by balancing a large, several-volume Russian dictionary and reciting the whole of *Endymion* in English. After several failures he was exhausted and sheepishly made do with a pocket Russian-English dictionary and a recitation of what he claimed was *Ode to a Nightingale* in Russian translation.

JUST SAY "NO"!

XVIII

Stir-fry the flag.

COMMENTARY

Roosevelt was put off by this stunt and, although he managed to perfunctorily cut Old Glory into short strips and complete the task in a large wok, he could not help blushing. Krinst may have meant to imply something about the war in the Pacific or the impending independence of Outer Mongolia, but scholars cannot agree.

𒀭𒁁𒂷𒁯𒌋
𒀸𒀸𒈨
𒅆𒀸𒂖
𒃻𒄿𒅅
𒌋𒁯𒁁𒀸
𒌤𒁹𒀾
𒅆𒀸𒁁𒃶𒅅
𒈠𒁯𒀸𒅅𒁁
𒄷𒅗𒈨
𒌤𒁹𒀾

MASTICATE A RUBBER BAND!

XIX

Construct a five-by-five word square.

COMMENTARY

This stunt took Churchill several hours to complete. Unfortunately his successful attempt does not survive and we are left with only a few preliminary failures:

```
P R O S E     P L U M S     C R A B S
O I L E D     L A B I A     L I N E N
E C O L E     U B U L Y     A L I B I
S C I O N     M I E O N     S L O O P
Y O L K S     B A R N S     S E N P S
```

DRINK AND DRIVE!

XX

Moo for entertainment purposes.

COMMENTARY

Once again, Churchill spared no effort in his animal impersonation; down on all fours, he lowed solemnly.

POLISH YOUR SOCKS!

XXI

Prepare to encounter a Rumanian.

COMMENTARY

Stalin first claimed that he was well prepared to encounter a Rumanian, but it soon became apparent that he believed that he needed only to shout in Russian to be understood. Churchill and Roosevelt convinced him to memorize a few helpful phrases.

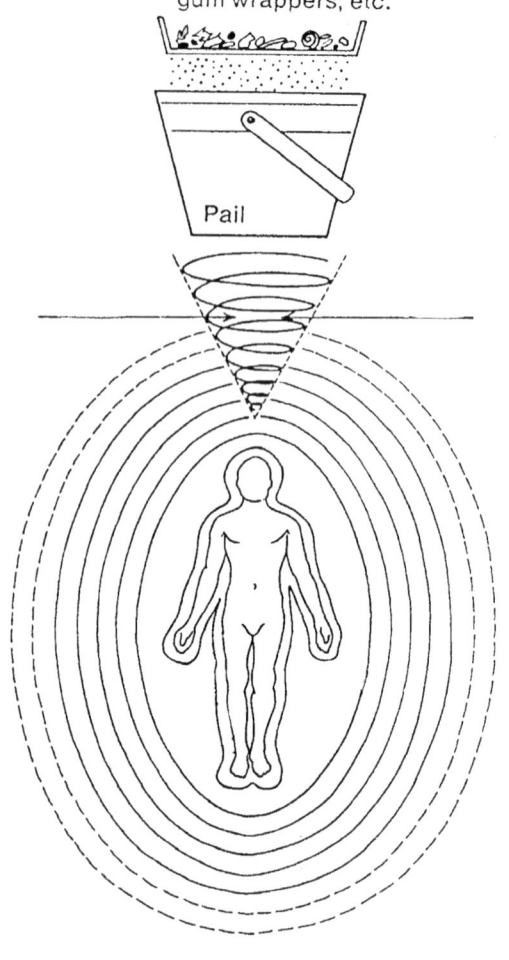

BARK FOR JESUS!

XXII

Filibuster the conclusion of this stunt.

COMMENTARY

The problematic nature of this stunt engendered a long philosophical conversation and, although Roosevelt and Stalin frequently expressed their exasperation at Churchill's semantic hair-splitting, the Englishman did manage to keep them engaged for some hours.

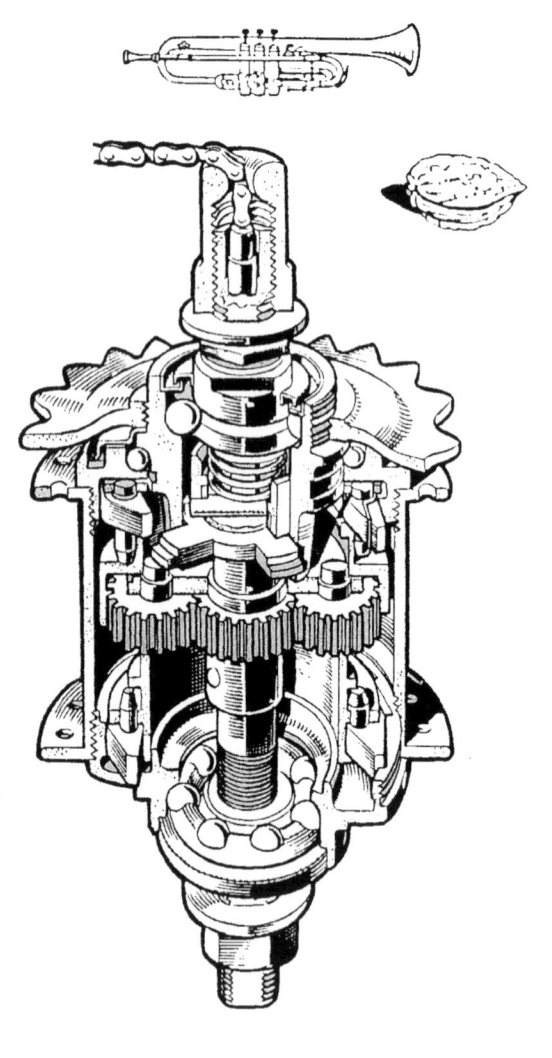

SPARE NOT THE ROD!

XXIII

Diligently eat deceitful meat with a ruler.

COMMENTARY

The "deceitful meat" agreed upon was a turkey stuffed with pebbles and gum wrappers. Roosevelt cut and consumed several pieces with a metal ruler (English system).

Sein oder nicht sein,
das ist die Frage

PINCH YOUR BUNS!

XXIV

Refuse to perform this stunt.

COMMENTARY

This stunt was not performed at the Yalta Conference.

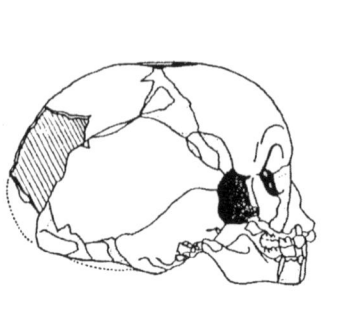

BREAK THE MOLD!

XXV

Kneel and spread peanut butter and jelly on a hymnal.

COMMENTARY

Churchill followed the directions demurely as Stalin chuckled thoughtlessly.

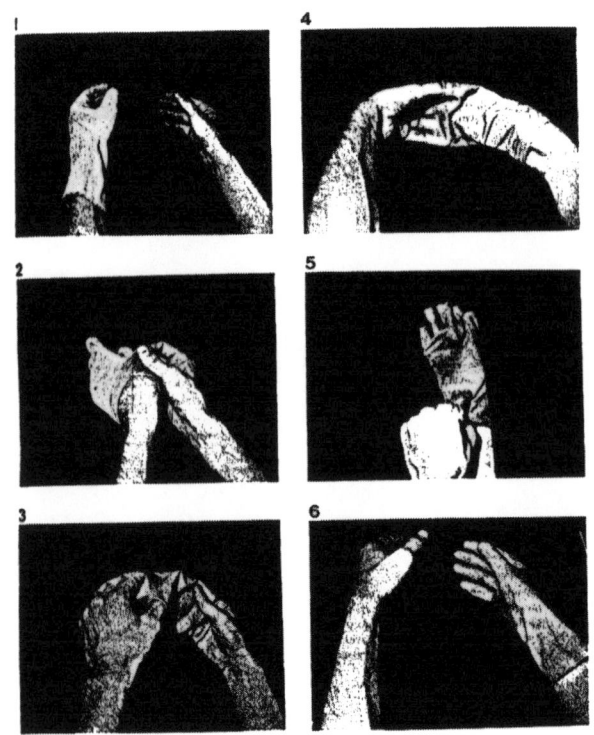

SWEAR YOU'LL ALWAYS LOVE ME!

XXVI

Croon and lasso a balloon.

COMMENTARY

After many clumsy attempts, Churchill received some helpful pointers from Roosevelt. He soon roped the necessary item and did a passable Bing Crosby.

BREAK BREAD

WITH A SWEEPER!

XXVII

Commemorate your solitude with a parade.

COMMENTARY

Stalin retired to a separate room for this stunt. Churchill later reported that he had heard the Soviet leader stamping and whistling "The Song of the Volga Boatmen."

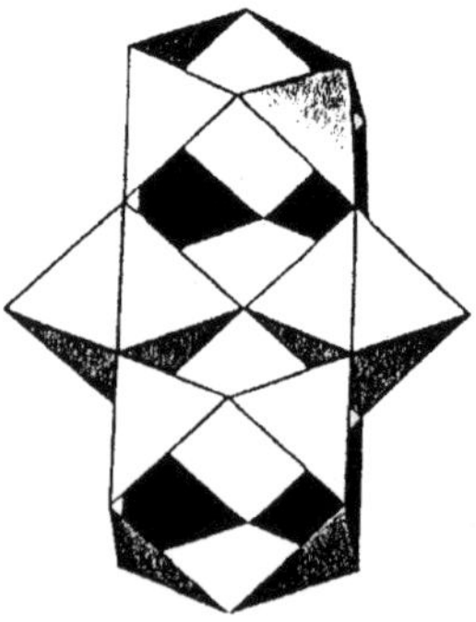

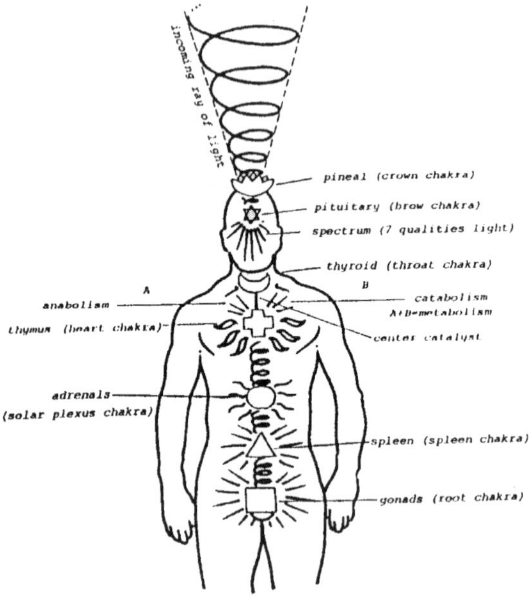

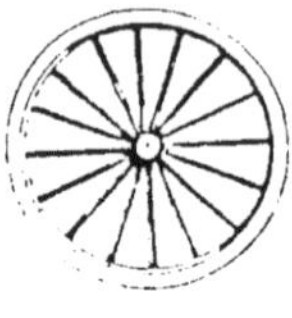

START SMOKING!

XXVIII

Extol the virtues of a banana.

COMMENTARY

Stalin pontificated at length upon the origins of the banana in "sweet Mother Russia" and recited absurd figures for crop production which kept, he claimed, "an army of the proletariat fed, fat, and happy."

কত অজানারে জানাইলে তুমি,
কত ঘরে দিলে ঠাঁই---
দূরকে করিলে নিকট বন্ধু,
পরকে করিলে ভাই।
পুরানো আবাস ছেড়ে যাই যবে
মনে ভেবে মরি কী জানি কী হবে,
নূতনের মাঝে তুমি পুরাতন
সে কথা যে ভুলে যাই
দূরকে করিলে নিকট বন্ধু,
পরকে করিলে ভাই।

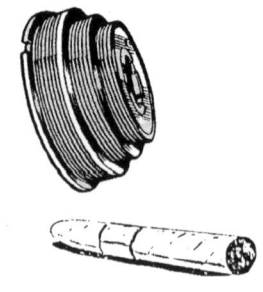

BRUSH UP ON YOUR

PROTOPLASM!

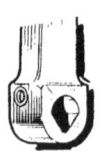

XXIX

Tickle the ivories with a feather duster.

COMMENTARY

After lecturing on the virtues of the folk idiom, Stalin thwacked the keys of the Steinway with the handle of the prescribed instrument.

Selected Works by Alvin Krinst

Dance

The Jazz Age of Haroun Al Rashid

Dramatic Works

Caviar
Dudley, the Frog of Pendmorton
Much Thumping About Sumping
The Pickle Eaters

Fiction

Alexia
No Smoking
Pale Soliloquy
Tight Frog

Music

Sleep Is My Banana
Murphy's Tweezer

Poetry

Bitching About Henbane
Clasp the Armoured Molecule
Dante's *Inferno*
DLLL's Ode to a Life of Affordable Pleasures
Flaming Putty
GIGFY
The Rube Goldberg Variations

Books from Sagging Meniscus Press

AARON ANSTETT
Moreover

WHEELER ANTABANEZ
The Old Asylum and Other Stories

LAURA DAVENPORT
An Occasional History

JACK FOLEY
The Tiger and Other Tales

MATTHEW GASDA
Orchid Elegy

TYLER GORE
My Life of Crime

CHARLES HOLDEFER
Dick Cheney in Shorts

ALVIN KRINST
The Yalta Stunts

ROY LISKER
In Memoriam Einstein
Lincoln Center in July and Other Stories

J.F. MAMJJASOND & FAFNIR FINKELMEYER
Hoptime

STEPHEN MOLES
The Most Wretched Thing Imaginable

M.J. NICHOLLS
The House of Writers
The Quiddity of Delusion

JOSEPH D. REICH
The Rituals of Mummification

CHRISTOPHER CARTER SANDERSON
The Too-Brief Chronicle of Judah Lowe

JACOB SMULLYAN
Dribble
Errata

RAYMOND M. SMULLYAN
A Mixed Bag: Jokes, Puzzles, Riddles and Memorabilia

JOHN TYNAN
Voice Lessons and Other Poems

FAY WEBERN
The Button Thief of East Fourteenth Street